TIM THE TIME-TRAVELING PORCUPINE

MAGIC E AND THE LONG I SOUND

By BLAKE HOENA

Illustrations by LUKE FLOWERS

Music by MARK OBLINGER

♪♫
CANTATA
LEARNING

WWW.CANTATALEARNING.COM

CANTATA
LEARNING

Published by Cantata Learning
1710 Roe Crest Drive
North Mankato, MN 56003
www.cantatalearning.com

A note to educators and librarians from the publisher: Cantata Learning has provided the following data to assist in book processing and suggested use of Cantata Learning product.

Publisher's Cataloging-in-Publication Data
Prepared by Librarian Consultant: Ann-Marie Begnaud
Library of Congress Control Number: 2016938095
    Tim the Time-Traveling Porcupine : Magic E and the Long I Sound
    Series: Read, Sing, Learn
    By Blake Hoena
    Illustrations by Luke Flowers
    Music by Mark Oblinger
    Summary: The wizard Magic E teaches readers how the silent e changes words like pin to pine, giving them a long I sound, in this outlandish story set to music.
    ISBN: 978-1-63290-794-3 (library binding/CD)
Suggested Dewey and Subject Headings:
    Dewey: E FIC
    LCSH Subject Headings: Wizards – Juvenile humor. | Wizards – Songs and music – Texts. | Wizards – Juvenile sound recordings.
    Sears Subject Headings: Magic. | Phonetics. | School songbooks. | Children's songs. | Jazz music.
    BISAC Subject Headings: JUVENILE FICTION / Fantasy & Magic. | JUVENILE FICTION / Stories in Verse. | JUVENILE FICTION / Humorous Stories.

Book design and art direction: Tim Palin Creative
Editorial direction: Flat Sole Studio
Music direction: Elizabeth Draper
Music written and produced by Mark Oblinger

Printed in the United States of America in North Mankato, Minnesota.
122016   0339CGS17

ACCESS THE MUSIC!
SCAN CODE WITH MOBILE APP
CANTATALEARNING.COM

TIPS TO SUPPORT LITERACY AT HOME

WHY READING AND SINGING WITH YOUR CHILD IS SO IMPORTANT

Daily reading with your child leads to increased academic achievement. Music and songs, specifically rhyming songs, are a fun and easy way to build early literacy and language development. Music skills correlate significantly with both phonological awareness and reading development. Singing helps build vocabulary and speech development. And reading and appreciating music together is a wonderful way to strengthen your relationship.

READ AND SING EVERY DAY!

TIPS FOR USING CANTATA LEARNING BOOKS AND SONGS DURING YOUR DAILY STORY TIME

1. As you sing and read, point out the different words on the page that rhyme. Suggest other words that rhyme.

2. Memorize simple rhymes such as Itsy Bitsy Spider and sing them together. This encourages comprehension skills and early literacy skills.

3. Use the questions in the back of each book to guide your singing and storytelling.

4. Read the included sheet music with your child while you listen to the song. How do the music notes correlate to the words of the song?

5. Sing along on the go and at home. Access music by scanning the QR code on each Cantata book, or by using the included CD. You can also stream or download the music for free to your computer, smartphone, or mobile device.

Devoting time to daily reading shows that you are available for your child. Together, you are building language, literacy, and listening skills.

Have fun reading and singing!

Have you heard of the Magic E? When added to the end of some words, it changes their vowel sound. For example, *pin* becomes *pine* and *kit* becomes *kite*. Sometimes Magic E is called the Silent E because it does this trick without making a sound.

Now Al-la-ke-zee! Ke-zi-ke-zie! What can the wizard Magic E do with an *E*?

Turn the page to see! Remember to sing along!

Tim, the prickly porcupine,
and his friend Pip, the **snub-nosed swine**,
saw the wizard Magic E
perched up in a tall pine tree.

THE WONDROUS WORLD OF e

Magic E offered Tim a wish—
one thing he wanted could be his.
Tim wished to travel back in time,
to when the dinos were alive.

"Easy as can be," said Magic E.
Then he began to dance and sing.

"Al-la-ke-zee! Ke-zi-ke-zie!
I bit a bite of apple pie.

Al-la-ke-zee! Ke-zi-ke-zie!
I slid down a slide from high in the sky.

Al-la-ke-zee! Ke-zi-ke-zie!
With an *E*, I'll turn Tim into time."

11

The wizard began to twirl his wand and then with a **flick** of his wrist— poof!

Tim got his **time-traveling** wish.

Next, Magic E offered Pip a wish—
one thing Pip wanted would be his.
Pip had hoped to play a pipe,
to make his friends sing and smile
so bright.

"Easy as can be," said Magic E.
Then he began to dance and sing.

"Al-la-ke-zee! Ke-zi-ke-zie!
I bit a bite of apple pie.

Al-la-ke-zee! Ke-zi-ke-zie!
I slid down a slide from high in the sky.

Al-la-ke-zee! Ke-zi-ke-zie!
With an *E*, I'll turn Pip into pipe."

17

The wizard began to twirl his wand and then with a flick of his wrist—
poof!

Pip got his pipe-playing wish.

19

"Al-la-ke-zee! Ke-zi-ke-zie!
I bit a bite of apple pie.

Al-la-ke-zee! Ke-zi-ke-zie!
I slid down a slide from high in the sky.

Al-la-ke-zee! Ke-zi-ke-zie!

With an *E*, I'll turn Tim into time.

Al-la-ke-zee! Ke-zi-ke-zie!

With an *E*, I'll turn Pip into pipe."

21

SONG LYRICS
Tim the Time-Traveling Porcupine

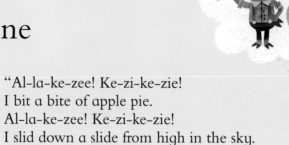

Tim, the prickly porcupine,
and his friend Pip, the snub-nosed swine,
saw the wizard Magic E
perched up in a tall pine tree.

Magic E offered Tim a wish—
one thing he wanted could be his.
Tim wished to travel back in time,
to when the dinos were alive.

"Easy as can be," said Magic E.
Then he began to dance and sing.

"Al-la-ke-zee! Ke-zi-ke-zie!
I bit a bite of apple pie.
Al-la-ke-zee! Ke-zi-ke-zie!
I slid down a slide from high in the sky.
Al-la-ke-zee! Ke-zi-ke-zie!
With an E, I'll turn Tim into time."

The wizard began to twirl his wand
and then with a flick of his wrist—poof!
Tim got his time-traveling wish.

Next, Magic E offered Pip a wish—
one thing Pip wanted would be his.
Pip had hoped to play a pipe,
to make his friends sing and smile so bright.

"Easy as can be," said Magic E.
Then he began to dance and sing.

"Al-la-ke-zee! Ke-zi-ke-zie!
I bit a bite of apple pie.
Al-la-ke-zee! Ke-zi-ke-zie!
I slid down a slide from high in the sky.
Al-la-ke-zee! Ke-zi-ke-zie!
With an E, I'll turn Pip into pipe."

The wizard began to twirl his wand
and then with a flick of his wrist—poof!
Pip got his pipe-playing wish.

"Al-la-ke-zee! Ke-zi-ke-zie!
I bit a bite of apple pie.
Al-la-ke-zee! Ke-zi-ke-zie!
I slid down a slide from high in the sky.
Al-la-ke-zee! Ke-zi-ke-zie!
With an E, I'll turn Tim into time.
Al-la-ke-zee! Ke-zi-ke-zie!
With an E, I'll turn Pip into pipe."

Tim the Time-Traveling Porcupine

Jazz
Mark Oblinger

Verse
Tim, the prick-ly por-cu-pine, and his friend Pip, the snub-nosed swine, saw the wiz-ard Mag-ic E perched up in a tall pine tree.

Mag-ic E of-fered Tim a wish— one thing he want-ed could be his. Tim wished to trav-el back in time, to when the di-nos were a-live.

Pre Chorus
"Eas-y as can be," said Mag-ic E. Then he be-gan to dance and sing.

Chorus
"Al-la-ke-zee! Ke-zi-ke-zie! I bit a bite of ap-ple pie. Al-la-ke-zee! Ke-zi-ke-zie! I slid down a slide from high in the sky.

Al-la-ke-zee! Ke-zi-ke-zie! With an E, I'll turn Tim in-to time."

The wiz-ard be-gan to twirl his wand and then with a flick of his wrist— poof! Tim got his time-trav-el-ing wish.

Verse
Next, Magic E offered Pip a wish—one thing Pip wanted would be his.
Pip had hoped to play a pipe, to make his friends sing and smile so bright.

Pre Chorus
"Easy as can be," said Magic E.
Then he began to dance and sing.

Chorus
"Al-la-ke-zee! Ke-zi-ke-zie! I bit a bite of apple pie.

Al-la-ke-zee! Ke-zi-ke-zie! I slid down a slide from high in the sky.

Al-la-ke-zee! Ke-zi-ke-zie! With an E, I'll turn Pip into pipe."

The wizard began to twirl his wand and then with a flick of his wrist—poof!
Pip got his pipe-playing wish.

Coda

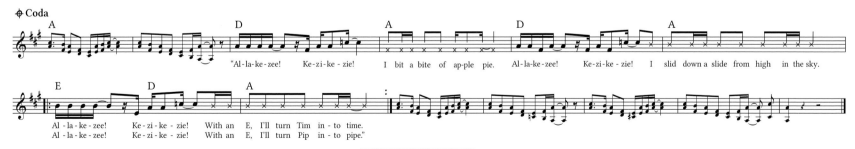

"Al-la-ke-zee! Ke-zi-ke-zie! I bit a bite of ap-ple pie. Al-la-ke-zee! Ke-zi-ke-zie! I slid down a slide from high in the sky.

Al-la-ke-zee! Ke-zi-ke-zie! With an E, I'll turn Tim in-to time.
Al-la-ke-zee! Ke-zi-ke-zie! With an E, I'll turn Pip in-to pipe."

23

GLOSSARY

flick—a small, quick movement

snub-nosed—having a flat nose like a pig's

swine—a pig

time-traveling—moving backward or forward in time

GUIDED READING ACTIVITIES

1. Pretend Magic E could give you a magical wish. Draw a picture of what you would wish for.

2. Add the Magic E to these words: *din*, *fin*, *shin*, and *tin*. What words did you make? Can you think of any other words to add the Magic E to?

3. In this book, Pip wanted to play the pipe to make his friends happy. What are some things you could do to make your friends happy? Try doing one of these things today!

TO LEARN MORE

Ballard, Peg. *Little Bit: The Sound of Short I*. Mankato, MN: Child's World, 2015.

Ghigna, Charles. *Adeline Porcupine*. North Mankato, MN: Capstone, 2016.

Hoena, Blake. *Rob the Mole and the Sneaky Gnome: Magic E and the Long O Sound*. North Mankato, MN: Cantata Learning, 2017.

Noyed, Robert B. *Smiles: The Sound of Long I*. Mankato, MN: Child's World, 2015.